24 Sept 2003

Dear Elizabeth

May all your days be ..

[signature]

MW00973835

Lisa the Weather Wonder™

The Sun in the Sky

By Lisa F. Mozer

Illustrated by Sean Parkes

Many thanks to my family and dear
friends who keep the faith.

www.lisamozer.com

I like the sun.
The sun gives us light.
The sun is not out at night.

The moon
is out at night.
The moon
is not very bright.

Sunrise is early
in the morning.
I get up early
in the morning
to see the sun rise.

The sun is a star.
The sun is round.
The sun is in the sky.

I like the sun.
The sun gives us light.

You should never stare at the sun.
The sun is so bright,
the light from the sun
can hurt your eyesight.

The heat from the bright sun
feels warm on my skin.
Heat feels good,
but I cannot see the heat.

Heat from the sun is invisible.
That means you cannot see heat
with your eyes.
Heat is invisible.

8

Where I live, in the summertime,
heat from the sun is very hot.
I do not need to wear a coat.
I do not need to wear a sweater.

I always wear my shoes outside.
My dad says, "Never go outside
without shoes on your feet."

If I stay outside for a long time,
I can get a suntan.
The heat from the sun turns
the color of my skin darker.

If I stay outside too long,
I might get a sunburn.
A sunburn can hurt.
"Ouch!"

Sometimes when I go outside to play,
I do not see the sun.

Sometimes when I go outside to play,
I see clouds all over the sky.

Some clouds are high
in the sky.

Some clouds are smooth
and cover all of the sky
way, way, way up high!

Some clouds
are low in the sky.

Some clouds
are white.
Some clouds
have dark and gray shadows.

I do not have
a shadow on
a cloudy day.

The sky is cloudy.

Clouds that are
low in the sky
are lumpy and bumpy
and can make it rain.

I look up at the sky and see
the dark clouds rushing by.
I run as fast as I can.
I run inside and stay nice and dry.

I like to look out my window.
I watch the rain
come down from the sky.

Rain can drop
in big wet spots.

Rain can pour
like a bath shower.

You can feel rain
on your skin.
Rain is water.

Rain feels wet.

Rain, rain, rain
makes everything outside
wet, wet, wet.

Sometimes when the lumpy bumpy
clouds bring rain,
I hear thunder.

Thunder is loud
like a big crash.
"KA-BOOOOM!"

If you hear thunder,
you might see
lightning in the sky.

When I hear thunder,
I stay away from the windows.
I am scared of lightning.

Lightning is electric.
Lightning lights up a dark sky.

It is very dark
outside after sunset.

The End.

Lisa The Weather Wonder Inc.
The author, Lisa Mozer, is a broadcast
meteorologist, public speaker and advocate
for advancing education in meteorology and
aviation. Lisa encourages young readers to
have fun learning about weather.
For more information on
Lisa The Weather Wonder books, visit
our web site at
www.lisamozer.com

For more information on Sean Parkes,
the illustrator, visit his web site at
www.seanparkes.com